New Moon

Money!

How to Get It, Spend It, and Save It

The New Moon Books Girls Editorial Board

Flynn Berry · Lauren Calhoun · Ashley Cofell
Morgan Fykes · Katie Hedberg · Elizabeth Larsson
Priscilla Mendoza · Julia Peters-Axtell · Caitlin Stern

CROWN PUBLISHERS, INC.   NEW YORK

For every girl who has been determined to gain independence
and power through work and money

Material on pages 63–64 by Barbara Riedel Sheedy originally appeared in *New Moon* magazine.

Text copyright © 2000 by New Moon Publishing, Inc.

All rights reserved. No part of this book may be reproduced or transmitted in any form or by any means, electronic or mechanical, including photocopying, recording, or by any information storage and retrieval system, without permission in writing from the publisher.

Published by Crown Publishers, a division of Random House, Inc.,
201 East 50th Street, New York, New York 10022.

CROWN and colophon are trademarks of Random House, Inc.

www.randomhouse.com/kids

Library of Congress Cataloging-in-Publication Data
New moon: money / New Moon Books Girls Editorial Board.—1st ed.
p. cm.
Based on New moon magazine.
Includes bibliographical references.
Summary: Girls discuss the importance and usefulness of money in their lives
and some ways to earn money now and in the future.
ISBN 0-517-88585-9 (tr. pbk.) — ISBN 0-517-88586-7 (lib. bdg.)
1. Money—Juvenile literature. 2. Finance, Personal—Juvenile literature. [1. Finance, Personal.
2. Moneymaking projects.] I. Title: Money.
HG221.5.N48   2000
322.24'055—dc21   99-046643

Printed in the United States of America
February 2000

10 9 8 7 6 5 4 3 2 1
First Edition

New Moon is a registered trademark of New Moon Publishing, Inc.

CONTENTS

CHAPTER ONE
What Money *Can* Buy
1

CHAPTER TWO
Working Girl
17

CHAPTER THREE
How to Manage Your Money
51

CHAPTER FOUR
Fun with Money
71

CHAPTER FIVE
Finding Out More About Money
80

The folks who made this book want to thank all the people who gave such enthusiastic help and who believe so strongly in Listening to Girls!

⭐

The Girls Editorial Board of *New Moon: The Magazine for Girls and Their Dreams,* the girls who read and create *New Moon* magazine, the New Moon Publishing team, and our parents.

⭐

Jennifer Cecil, Sheila Eldred, Seth Godin Productions, Bridget Grosser, Mavis Gruver, Debra Kass Orenstein, Joe Kelly, Nia Kelly, Erin Lyons, Jason Mandell, Deb Mylin, Sarah Silbert, Barbara Stretchberry, and Ann Weinerman.

⭐

Our colleagues at Lark Productions: Robin Dellabough, Lisa DiMona, and Karen Watts.

⭐

And our friends at Crown Publishing: Simon Boughton, Andrea Cascardi, Michelle Gengaro-Kokmen, Nancy Hinkel, and Isabel Warren-Lynch.

Note from *New Moon*'s Founder

New Moon is a magazine that gives girls the power to believe in ourselves, to help us stand up for what we think is right, and, most of all, to let us just be girls. *New Moon* sends a message that makes a girl feel, "However I am, I'm okay." *New Moon* describes girls who take action when things are unfair, instead of keeping quiet. And *New Moon* is a fun, safe place where girls know that they are not alone.

New Moon: The Magazine for Girls and Their Dreams is an international, advertising-free bimonthly that is edited BY girls between ages 8 and 14. The recipient of dozens of awards, *New Moon* was twice named winner of the Parents' Choice Foundation Gold Award—the only child-edited magazine ever to win that honor. Begun in 1993, *New Moon* is a girl-driven alternative to magazines and other media that focus on how girls look. *New Moon*'s slant is that makeup, boys, and fashion are important to girls, but they represent maybe three degrees of a girl's life. *New Moon* focuses on the other 357 degrees of a thinking girl's life.

This series of New Moon Books continues that mission. Our books talk about real issues and real girls. They don't say, "This is how you have to be." Instead, they share girls' experiences, feelings, and ideas. Just like *New Moon* magazine, New Moon Books are created BY girls. We chose nine *New Moon* readers from all over the country, including Alaska and Hawaii, Minnesota and New York, to work on the books. They range in age from 10 to 14 and represent home school, public school, and private school. White, Black, Filipino, and Asian, these girls have done a marvelous job, as we knew they would.

In this book, they write about the roles of money and work, paid and volunteer, as sources of power in our lives. Working with Robin Dellabough of Lark Productions and Joe Kelly of New Moon Publishing, they explore the jobs and careers girls and women can have, attitudes toward money, and financial skills every girl should know. Of course, they also describe lots of ways money, and even work, can be entertaining, fascinating, and fun!

We think you'll love this book because it's about how real girls are inspired to become empowered through work. So get ready to find out more about money and independence by Listening to Girls, which is our favorite thing to do!

Molly McKinnon
Editor, *New Moon: The Magazine for Girls and Their Dreams*

Nancy Gruver
Founder & Publisher, New Moon Publishing

Note from the New Moon Books Girls Editorial Board

We are very proud to be the Girls Editorial Board for these books. We hope that they will help other girls feel good about themselves and their abilities. Like you, we are strong, spirited girls. We got together at a hotel in New York to start creating the books. We had an awesome weekend, where we worked hard and played hard. We came up with ideas for most of the material in the books and had a say in everything that went into them. We chose topics that we wanted to write about, too. After that, we worked on the books and with each other over the Internet. And when each book was almost finished, we edited it and said what should change. All in all, it was a pretty amazing experience!

We appreciate New Moon's approach and feel lucky to be reaching more girls through this series of books. Sure, some of us may like boys and putting on makeup, but we also enjoy playing sports, spending time with our friends, learning about international happenings, reading, writing, and all of the other exciting things the world has to offer. That's why we researched and wrote about friendship, earning money, reading, writing, and sports — things that are important to girls in their lives. We found, in the United States and around the world, girls with competence and self-respect. We hope that you will find, in their experiences, the inspiration that every girl needs. Girls are so much more than clothes and diets; we are individuals with views and ideas, energy and talent. New Moon is our voice. Add yours and let us be heard!

Flynn Berry, age 11, New York
Lauren Calhoun, age 13, Hawaii
Ashley Cofell, age 10, Minnesota
Morgan Fykes, age 12, Washington, D.C.
Katie Hedberg, age 11, Minnesota

Elizabeth Larsson, age 12, New Jersey
Priscilla Mendoza, age 11, California
Julia Peters-Axtell, age 14, Minnesota
Caitlin Stern, age 13, Alaska

What Money Can Buy

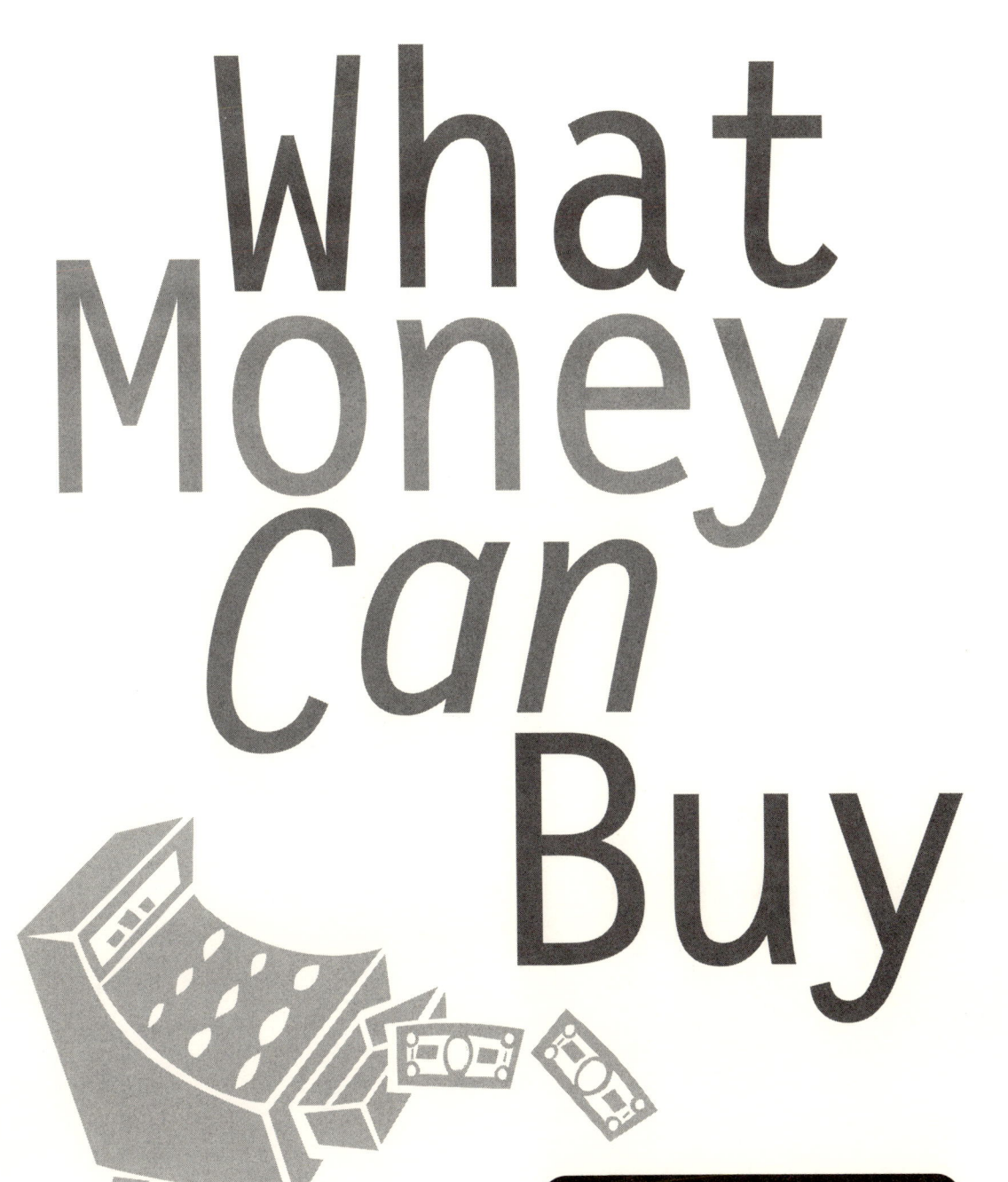

CHAPTER ONE

What Money *Can* Buy

One day you walk past The Gap and see the perfect pair of jeans. You run inside and try them on. They fit exactly. What a setup, right? Until you look at the price tag: $40. Gulp. You haven't got that much because you just spent all your savings on a used bike. Wait, the day is saved. There's that baby-sitting job you heard about: 8 hours at $5 per hour = $40 exactly. But remember? You turned the job down because you have a major test to study for.

Hmmmm...what's a girl to do?

The great news is that you *have* a choice! For centuries, women and girls didn't. We were treated as property and not allowed to make our own decisions. This is still true for many modern women. Saudi Arabian women are not allowed to drive. Many Pakistani women must marry the men their fathers choose.

For many others, however, this legacy of inequality is being brushed aside, with the help of the capable hands of strong women. We can now grow up knowing that all people are equal. We can grow up to be whatever we want, as long as we try hard enough. We can earn our own money at our own jobs as mechanics, engineers, lawyers, teachers, writers, artists, doctors, or scientists, or in any other profession. We have the independence to discover for ourselves our likes and dislikes. We have the power to make our own choices.

Dreams

I sit and think about the future
And what it means to me,
As I dream and wait and wonder and listen
Beneath a tall oak tree.

I might be a star on Broadway,
My days filled with fortune and fame,
Or I might not be what I want to be,
And my days will be filled with shame.

I could grow up to be anything!
About anything there is to be.
As I dream and wait and wonder and listen
Beneath a tall oak tree.

—Jarrett, age 11, Georgia

What Money *Can* Buy

Knowing how to make, save, invest, and spend money is a vital part of a modern girl's life. We don't know about you, but we don't want to be dependent on relatives, spouses, or friends all our lives. We want to survive and thrive on our own. Being able to make and keep money gives you the independence to pay off debts, rent or buy a place to live, and provide yourself with food and clothes. It gives you the power to help and support others or donate to a cause you believe in. It's a great tool!

Remember how when you were little, everyone was always asking you what you wanted to be when you grew up? What did you say? People still ask us that question. What would you say now? When you grow up, will you get a job? If so, will you work only for money so that you can enjoy yourself in your time off? Or will you love your work so much that you'll *want* to do it, even if the pay is low? Will you look for a job that is both high-paying and personally rewarding? Maybe, if you get married, your husband will support you. That's cool, but almost all women end up working at some time during their lives — to support their families or themselves.

When we're out in the world working, we can have power, impact, and independence. If we get paid for the work we do, we have money!

What Money Can Buy

All of us like having...

power — knowing that we're making a difference in the world;

independence — the freedom to share our beliefs and dreams;

and at least a bit of **money** — to pay for the things we need and want.

How do we get these things? We work for them. And that's what this book is really about.

Do what you love, the money will follow.
—Marsha Sinetar

Fast Forward

Take a minute now to fantasize about your future. Do you have any idea of how much it costs to support yourself? Whether you get an allowance or ask your parents for your entertainment money, you should realize that there are lots of reasons families dig into their pockets.

One common technique families use for making sure they don't spend more than they have is a budget. There are many forms of budgeting. Putting aside half of all of your income (income is how much cash you get over a certain period of time—daily, weekly, annually, etc.) for a pair of shoes until you save enough money for them is budgeting. An adult budget would divide expenses the same way, but it would label needs as "fixed expenses" and wants as "nonfixed expenses." Fixed expenses include house mortgage or rent; car, home, and health insurance; and taxes. Nonfixed expenses include entertainment, clothes, vacations, gifts, and telephones. Adults use the money left over, or "disposable income," to pay for nonfixed expenses. (For definitions of more financial terms, check the glossary on page 84.)

> *Wealth consists not in having great possessions but in having few wants.*
> —Esther de Waal

Many families also are careful to put aside money each week, or each month, for savings. Sometimes the money is taken out of a paycheck before the wage earner even sees it and is deposited automatically in a savings account. Some families prefer to set aside money every week and

What Money *Can* Buy

take it to the bank themselves. It could go to general savings or to an education fund for each child. What matters is that there is money put aside on a regular basis.

For a reality check, sit down with your parents while they do their bills. See where their paychecks actually go every week or every month. What do they pay for weekly? Some things could be child care, groceries, dry cleaning, and gas for the car. A weekly bill might be for your music teacher or karate class, or even your pizza money. Each month, your parents probably write out checks for the rent or the mortgage and for the telephone, heating, and electric bills. Other common expenses include the newspaper delivery service, cable TV, and online providers. Some families pay their insurance bills every few months, while others pay one large amount once a year. Insurance covers not only the house and car but also your family's health, so that if someone gets critically ill, all your savings aren't used up. And some parents pay taxes every three months instead of once a year, especially if they are in business for themselves.

Of course, sometimes no matter how carefully you budget to put away savings, you won't have enough cash for a major purchase. Things like cars, houses, and college educations are some of the major expenses you will probably

What Money Can Buy

have in your life that may require you to take out some form of a loan.

A special loan, known as a mortgage, helps you buy a home. To get a mortgage from a bank, the bank will want to see how much money you earn at your job on a weekly or monthly basis, the amount of money you've saved, and other assets that you may have (like stocks, bonds, or other investments). Usually a bank will lend you about 80 percent of the purchase price, provided you meet its requirements. And usually banks want the buyer to put down the remaining 20 percent.

Another type of loan is an automobile loan. In some ways, it's like a mortgage, except it's for a car. You are expected to put down about 20 percent of the car's price, and the lender will let you borrow the remaining 80 percent. You can take out a car loan from a bank, or you can work out the arrangements directly with the car dealership. Let's say you took out a $15,000 car loan at 8 percent interest for a period of 3 years. That would mean monthly car payments of $470.

That 8 percent interest is the rate the bank charges you to borrow money. (It can also refer to the opposite: the rate you are *paid* for keeping funds on deposit.)

If you took out a $100,000 30-year loan at 8 percent,

you would have a $734 monthly payment to make. A $200,000 loan on the same terms would mean a $1,468 monthly payment.

Credit cards are another way to take out a loan, even if they don't look like it. Basically, a bank or a credit card company lends you money to make your purchases, and you are expected to pay it back when you get your monthly credit card bill. Credit cards offer convenience (sometimes a store won't accept a personal check, and you don't have to carry large amounts of cash). Be careful not to keep a running balance on a credit card, since the bank or credit card company charges high interest on that amount. Many banks and credit card companies also charge a yearly fee, usually ranging from $15 to $50, so take your time to shop around for a credit card without a fee.

Debit cards are another way to pay for things with plastic instead of "real" money or checks. They work like credit cards, but there's one big difference: There is no interest charged on the money you spend. Instead, it is deducted automatically from your checking account. So you get the convenience of a credit card without the danger of overspending that a credit card might encourage. If you're under 18, you can't get a debit card in your own name, but some parents get cards for their kids.

What Money *Can* **Buy**

The average American family of four spends $84 a week on groceries, according to the Food Marketing Institute.

Strolling Down the Aisles

Next time your family goes food shopping, take along a notebook or calculator and figure out exactly where the weekly food budget goes. How much money do you spend on cold cereal, sodas, and snacks? How much does it really cost to prepare well-balanced meals and keep the pantry stocked? When you see what it costs to throw in that extra package of cookies or candy bars and how quickly it adds up, you may want to rethink some of your eating and buying habits.

In the next chapter, we'll look at ways you can work to earn money, gain experience, have fun, and maybe even help the world. But before you get specific, think about what you'd most like to do with your time and what you'd be good at by filling in the following section — created by a girl, of course!

POINT OF VIEW: *Weaving Your Dreams into Your Life*

What do you love to do? Why do you love it? By analyzing your favorite activities, what can you learn about yourself?

More than you think!

A lot of people don't realize that the things they love doing hold the seeds of what they are good at. They don't realize that by exploring what they love, they can learn lots about themselves and what they need in order to have a happy life. You can even build your whole life around the things you love to do!

For instance, I love to draw. I love to be in charge of what I draw, creating something from beginning to end. I love colors. I also love to concentrate, and I like the way my hand moves and the way my body is involved. I like to transform the things I see around me into my own artistic vision. I love it when people praise me and appreciate what I draw.

See how much you can learn about yourself from one thing that you love to do? It doesn't matter if you love looking out the window, playing with your dog, or enjoying the outdoors. Looking closely enough at it will help you learn about yourself.

Fill out the "My Perfect Life" section below. Don't imagine

just practical ideas for your future job or career. Really look at what you want to do, even if it doesn't seem practical. When you get to "five years later," try to imagine how your career has changed and what is different. Be open to possibilities and expect that your original dream might change directions. Don't lock up your hope and imagination. Let your dreams become your future!

My Perfect Life

One thing I really love to do:
Why I love it:
My exciting life and career based on this:
Imagine five years later. What am I doing now?
What have I discovered about myself from doing this exercise?

Here is how I filled out my own "My Perfect Life":

One thing I really love to do: DRAWING
Why I love it:
Making choices and being in charge.
Drawing feels good physically.
Creating something from beginning to end.
Color.

Making beauty.

Concentration.

Getting praise.

Using my imagination.

My exciting life and career based on drawing:

My first career would be to sell drawings. I'd work with my friends, drawing what I see and being outside. I would help people use their imagination. I might have drawing classes for children. I would travel around, drawing and going to museums. I would live at the beach, in the house my grandparents owned.

Imagine five years later:

I begin to sell drawings to museums. I am famous. I live in the house where I grew up. I collect fragile things. I give the world beautiful things to see—colors, textures, and imagination. I would have drawing classes open to the public.

What have I discovered about myself from doing this exercise?

In my life I want to do work that allows me to use my imagination. I like to help other people use colors and imagination. I learned that I want to be famous and help others. I like being in charge of my life and might work best if I am the boss. I like using all my senses and concentrating. I like putting my own way of seeing things into the work I am doing.

—Lily, age 9, Pennsylvania

What Money *Can* **Buy**

Read about one woman who found a way to combine what she loves with making a living.

HIGH PROFILE: ANN REED

Ann Reed is a musician, a role model, and a giving person. Her career is being a singer, guitar player, and songwriter, and she does these things in a way that shows that she cares about women and about being herself even while she is trying to earn money.

It's hard to describe her music, but it comes closest to folk music. One of her most famous songs is "Heroes." It's about women heroes like Sojourner Truth, Susan B. Anthony, and Harriet Tubman. It makes me think of the stories of the women I know about. Sometimes I get curious about the women I haven't heard of; then I ask or find out about them.

When I asked Ann how she started to be a musician, she said she had known she loved playing the guitar, singing, and writing since she was very young, but she didn't think anyone would *pay* her to do it! When she was a couple of years out of high school, she figured out that she could actually have a career and make her living by doing something she loved. She said that she could probably make more money if she played country or pop music, but she chose to play the music she loves and the music she writes, even if it won't make her rich. She doesn't like to have people telling her what she can play, what she should wear, where she can perform. That's why she didn't sign with a big recording label. Instead, she formed her own record company, called "A Major Label."

Ann even wrote a song about being herself when playing music, called "I'll Keep My Hat." In the song, she's meeting with someone in Nashville about a record contract. She bought a cowboy hat "to make it all seem real." Then the record contractor tells her to "put a cute dress on, dye your hair blonde, and get rid of the hat." She tells the record contractor, "I'm going back home, I'm never looking back.... You wouldn't know a good tune if it introduced itself to you.... I'll have better luck myself, and I can keep my hat."

By taking control of her own career, Ann is able to do many more things that make her feel really good. About twenty-five percent of her touring schedule consists of concerts for organizations that help women and children. She has done many shows to raise money for battered women's shelters, breast cancer research organizations, and AIDS research. She says, "Many of these concerts

What Money *Can* Buy

weren't very big — they might've had a hundred or two hundred people — and a major label wouldn't bother with attendance of that size."

I asked Ann Reed if she could give some tips for people who might want to be singers or songwriters. This is what she said:

1. Do it because you love it, not because you think you'll get rich.
2. Practice your instrument (this includes your voice) every day.... Hate to be clichéd, but it really, really does "make perfect."
3. Perform whenever you can when you start out. The more practice you have being in front of an audience, the better you will be as a performer.
4. Find others who are playing the same instrument, singing, or writing songs and who may be just a little more advanced than you are. You always learn from other musicians.

Ann Reed lives in Minneapolis. Her CDs and tapes can be found in the folk music sections of some record stores. For a catalog of her recordings, write to Turtlecub Productions, P.O. Box 8240, Minneapolis, Minnesota 55408.

—Ashley, age 10, Minnesota

Working Girl

HELP ★ WANTED

CHAPTER TWO

So you want to have some independence and not have to rely on your family for your spending money or savings. Great. Now what? How do you actually go about finding work that you're good at and would like to do?

There are three big questions to consider when you work for pay:

- ★ What are you able to do?
- ★ What do you want to get out of work?
- ★ How much money do you want to earn?

Start off by figuring out what your talents and skills are — and then be creative in looking for potential employers or starting your own business. Maybe you like to take care of children or pets, or run errands for older neighbors. Or maybe you're the more technological type and can design Web sites, write code, or test computer games. Then again, perhaps you're talented at art or calligraphy and would enjoy making simple party favors for kids' birthdays. The possibilities are endless if you think big!

But how do you actually find a job?

One way is to read through the local newspaper or *Pennysaver* (or any free community publication that comes to people's homes) — even a school newspaper, if it takes community and private ads — to see what kinds of jobs are being advertised.

Another helpful place to find job openings is the bulletin board of a community center, school, grocery store, church, or synagogue. Sometimes parents who are looking for baby-sitters, or people looking for house- and pet-sitters, will advertise this way.

What if you'd rather work for yourself? Decide whether you'd like to provide a service (pet grooming, yard work, grocery shopping for a disabled neighbor) or make a product (home-baked muffins, hand-painted silk scarves, personalized picture frames).

Try to have a pretty good idea of how long it takes you to do or make something so you can set a fair price for your time and effort. If you're making a product, also figure out how much the materials cost you (such as the baking ingredients for a batch of cupcakes, or paints and crafts supplies) so that you can price your product appropriately. Your profit is what you're left with after you've paid the costs of making something.

Working Girl

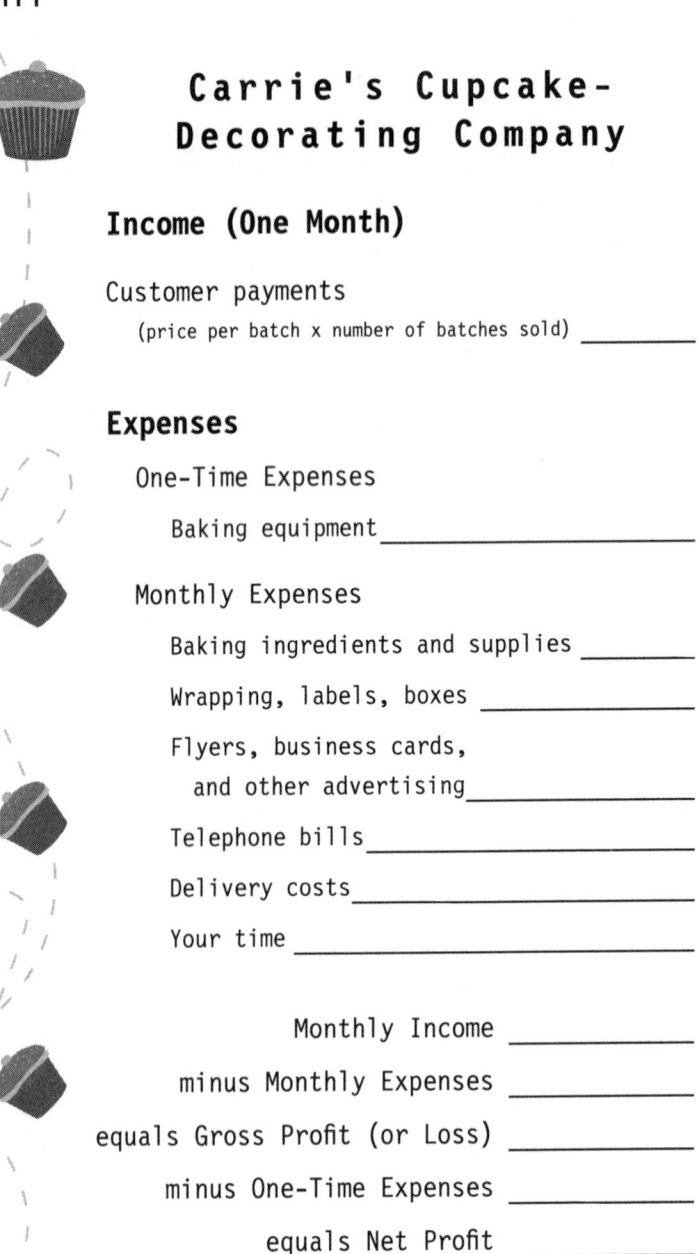

Carrie's Cupcake-Decorating Company

Income (One Month)

Customer payments
(price per batch x number of batches sold) _____

Expenses

One-Time Expenses

Baking equipment _____

Monthly Expenses

Baking ingredients and supplies _____

Wrapping, labels, boxes _____

Flyers, business cards,
and other advertising _____

Telephone bills _____

Delivery costs _____

Your time _____

Monthly Income _____
minus Monthly Expenses _____
equals Gross Profit (or Loss) _____
minus One-Time Expenses _____
equals Net Profit _____

Remember that jobs that sound the same aren't always the same. Buying and putting away the groceries for an older person who lives alone in a small apartment is a lot different from shopping for a family with three children that has a large kitchen, a pantry, and a basement storage closet. In some cases, you may be better off charging a basic price for a job, and in others, you may do better with an hourly rate.

Speaking of hourly rates, what about working at a store or a fast-food restaurant? In most states, you need to have something called "working papers." Working papers, which are usually available through your school's guidance office (or the guidance counselor will be able to tell you where to get them), basically tell an employer that you're legally old enough to work in a commercial business. To get working papers, you have to show a birth certificate and a Social Security number. The age varies from state to state (in some places you can get them at 14, in other places you have to wait until you are 15 or 16). Your age also may determine what kind of work you can be hired to do. For example, if you're hired at a supermarket at age 14, you may be able to be a bagger or a cashier, but you won't be allowed to work behind the deli counter with the meat slicers.

Working Girl

Finding Business

Are you open for business? Yes, but...Perhaps you're wondering how to get customers. One way of getting jobs is advertising.

Advertising is the most popular and common form of reeling in business. It's a way of informing people what you are offering. Advertising can include anything from business cards to an ad in your local newspaper.

Don't be afraid to market yourself. Print up three-by-five index cards with your first name, age, phone number, and a description of what you want to do (baby-sitting, errand running, yard work, etc.) and put them up around your town's bulletin boards — at the library, post office, supermarket, schools, and recreation centers. Be sure to ask your parents to tell everyone they know you're looking for work, too.

Priscilla has this advice: "If you are ready for business and ready to gather up new customers, create some flyers! On brightly colored paper, clearly jot down some basic, necessary information, such as what you are providing, where you can be reached, etc. Pass out flyers to your neighbors and post them on community bulletin boards."

> When someone calls to offer you a job at her or his home, be sure to have your parents check that this is a safe and comfortable situation. You don't want to put yourself in a position of working in a stranger's house without knowing something about her or him.

Getting Paid

"Money can be a delicate issue, but it doesn't have to be," Flynn says. "Some people, such as yours truly, find it embarrassing to state the price of their services. Unfortunately, I learned the hard way that a moment of embarrassment is much better than the alternative. When you aren't up-front about the cost, you may get rewarded with a bag of popcorn for your troubles, or other things undesirable under the circumstances." So our advice is to *always* find out how much you're going to be paid before you start work.

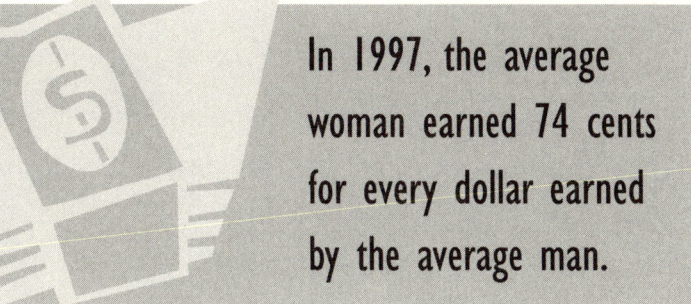

> In 1997, the average woman earned 74 cents for every dollar earned by the average man.

Working Girl

Ask a Girl

"I get plenty of jobs around my neighborhood, including baby-sitting, shoveling snow, pet-sitting, and cleaning. My problem is that I never know how much I'm going to be paid until the job's done. Also, sometimes people forget to pay me. What should I say?"

You need to take charge! Although it may seem awkward, people love it when you tell them how much money you want for a job. It takes all of the pressure off of them—they don't know how much to pay you otherwise. When someone forgets, gently remind him or her. You deserve money, and they know you do. Speak up!

Keeping Customers

When you get a job, the people you are working for expect you to be responsible. Why else would they leave their pets or children in your hands? You must live up to their expectations—or surpass them!

If you are baby-sitting, for example, show up at least ten

minutes early. That way the parents can give you last-minute instructions, you can ask questions, and they can get ready while you get acquainted with the children. Be dressed neatly and in clean clothes—no grungy flannel shirts. Appear crisp and professional.

When your clients talk to you, hold yourself straight and look them in the eye. Speak clearly and don't mumble. Smile and act responsible! Do not chew gum—don't even have gum!—or bite your nails, slouch, or say "whatever." Say "yes" or "no," or, if you don't know the answer to a question, say you'll have to discuss it with your parents and you'll call them back.

If you have to cancel, call at least four days before the job. If you absolutely must cancel after that, call up a responsible person and tell your client that you have a friend who would be willing to do the job in your place.

Finally, do the job as well as you can!

The Way Things Work

Now we're ready to describe a bunch of ways real girls and women have made real money.

First up is highly successful small-business owner *and* artist Emily Burdick.

Working Girl

HIGH PROFILE: EMILY BURDICK

At age 11, Emily Burdick of Houston, Texas, started her own jewelry business, called Emilina's Original Jewelry Designs. She was 13 when New Moon interviewed her.

New Moon: How did you start your business?

Emily Burdick: My aunt Beth helped me. She makes jewelry, too. She taught me how to make beaded eyeglass chains. After that, I started doing necklaces, and I kept going from there.

NM: What kind of jewelry do you make?

EB: "Y" necklaces, beaded chains with crosses and hearts at the end, turquoise bracelets, hair clips, and angel pins. I like making angel pins. It's neat mixing and matching pieces. The glue kind of makes you dizzy, though.

NM: Where do you sell your jewelry?

EB: At craft shows. And I sell angel pins at my grandparents' Catholic bookstore.

NM: What's the hardest thing about running your own business?

EB: I had to spend a lot of money to get started, and sometimes when I'm buying supplies, I go overboard. Also, at first I had a really hard time with publicity. Before I started giving my grandparents stuff, nobody had heard about me, and nobody was calling to make orders. I wasn't doing very well at all.

NM: How much money do you make selling your jewelry now?

EB: I usually make between $200 and $250 at a craft show. After paying for the supplies I used to make the jewelry I sold, my profit is about $150.

NM: Do you have to work a lot?

EB: Not too much. It depends on how much I have to make. I usually work right before a craft show, and that's about it. It takes me ten minutes to make an angel pin. A beaded necklace takes me between half an hour and forty-five minutes.

NM: Why do you like having a jewelry business?

EB: I like seeing what other people make, and I try to make new things, since making the same thing over and over again isn't very exciting. And going to the craft shows is fun.

NM: What have you learned about running a business?

EB: Of course, I've learned how to make jewelry. Besides that, I've learned a lot about how to mark prices.

NM: Do you have any advice for other girls who want to start a business?

EB: I picked something hard to do, because a lot of people here make jewelry. The easiest thing to do is to do something original. Try to find something that no one else is doing or that nobody wants to do. The most important thing is to find something that you like to do.

—Emma and Julia, ages 11 and 14, Minnesota

Gardening/Landscaping

It's the beginning of summer, and you're broke. Two of your friends have already snagged steady baby-sitting jobs, and another one is cleaning house for her grandmother's friend. The only job you can find is sorting files in your aunt's office, and who wants to be stuck inside when there's such great weather? So what do you do? How about planting nasturtiums and mowing the lawn for the garden-obsessed neighbor down the street?

Gardening/landscaping work gets you out in the sun, gives you exercise, and can pay up to $5 per hour. So if you work 2 hours a day, 4 days a week, that could mean up to $40. But it's not always a blast. Pulling weeds for hours gets monotonous, and spreading fertilizer could be the champion of the stinky jobs. You can learn a lot from the gardeners you work for, though, especially if you plan on having a garden of your own someday.

Try trading your time for something you want. Maybe you could plant and tend window boxes for a store and get a certain amount of credit there each week.

If you like being outside and learning about plants, look in your area for the serious gardeners who might need a hand. Parks around libraries or museums, and planters outside stores, can be possible places to work, too. It could be pretty cool to see a twig you planted turn into a huge tree one day. And almost everyone can use a little help in the garden.

Working Girl

Snow Shoveling

Every year when winter rolls around and announces itself with a storm, my friend and I haul out the snow shovels and go door-to-door offering our services as snow shovelers. One day, we worked for about two and a half hours and raked (or shoveled) in $75 each! Very profitable, but it doesn't snow very much here, so it is a rare day when I bundle up against the snow and venture outside. It is a good idea to hit the streets relatively early, about 9:30 or 10, so that you get all the jobs before other kids. But never go around before 8:30 — you don't want to wake people up and have them be cranky.

—Flynn, age 11, New York

Garage Sales

If you want fast cash and you have a lot of stuff lying around the house you don't want, a garage sale is for you. If you have a garage sale section in your newspaper, put in an ad with your address and a general idea of what you are selling. Then set up signs leading to your house so people can find it. Set your stuff out on a table (in neatly sorted piles and attractively arranged on hangers) and price your items with little tags. It's easier if you have a calculator to add up sales, plenty of change, and a money box to keep your money in.

—Lauren, age 13, Hawaii

Have a Car Wash!

Grab some friends, a hose, buckets, soap, wax, a few towels, some cardboard and bright markers, and a hot day, and have a fun soak-down while making money! First, get your bud(s) assembled and make some signs on cardboard. Keep them simple:

> CAR WASH!!!!!
> $5 per car, wax $2 extra.
> TODAY ONLY!!!!
> From 10 A.M.–3 P.M.
> Come to 33 Sycamore Lane.
> Refreshments and magazines
> to keep you entertained while you wait!

Place the signs near the place where you're washing the cars and in an easy-to-spot location that lots of cars drive

Working Girl

by. Have a bucket with soapy water, a few rags, a hose for rinsing off, and car wax ready before the first customers arrive. Cookies and magazines are optional but recommended. Agree on a price with your friends, and wait. Once the cars come, clear the price with their owners (better safe than sorry) and get sudsing. Most likely, it'll turn into an awesome water fight, but keep working while you're spraying. Have fun!

A Bookstore by and for Kids

If you ran a bookstore, what would you charge for each book? Who would you want to work for you? What kinds of jobs would there be?

At Public School 121, in the Bronx, New York, fourth- and fifth-grade students operate a bookstore for their school, with a little help from reading teacher Robin Cohen. The kids are the cashiers, stock clerks, security guards, and advertising executives.

They started the store because there are no bookstores in their neighborhood, and because many kids couldn't afford to buy new books anyway. P.S. 121's store charges only

POINT OF VIEW: The Eyes Have It

I started my eye-pillow business last year. An eye pillow is a silk (or any other fabric) pillow small enough to fit over your eyes, filled with tiny little flaxseeds. Now, you're probably wondering where in the world you can get flaxseed. My mom orders it in bulk from a health food store. You can also buy it in small packages. Flaxseed is sometimes used for cooking, which is why you can get it at a health food store.

My mom loved eye pillows and thought they would be easy to make. She had taught me how to sew, so she suggested we start a business. We tested different weights and amounts of flaxseeds and sizes of the pillow, and finally came up with the perfect eye pillow. Next, it was time to think of a name: Crystal Eyes. We sold these eye pillows to my mom's massage therapist, who then sold them to her clients. My business was started.

My mom helps me make the pillows. I get the money and put it into my savings account. The money I make is used to pay for sewing machine repairs, supplies, etc. After the eye pillows were a success at the massage therapist's office, she told a yoga teacher, and the yoga teacher got interested. I now sell the eye pillows to both the yoga teacher and the massage therapist.

The number of eye pillows that we sell each month varies, depending on whether it's near a holiday, what time of year it is, and how many eye pillows we sold in the last batch. I'm not sure yet how much of a profit I have made. The hardest part of my business is probably disciplining myself and making myself work. The business is a pretty nice size right now, small enough for me to be personal with my customers but big enough so that we make a profit.

It's really a great experience, owning a business. It improves my math skills, my people skills, and my sewing. I couldn't have done it without the help and encouragement of my mom. My advice to girls who want to start their own business is: Make sure that it sells something that people want to buy. Also, have a good time with whatever you do.

—Elizabeth, age 12, New Jersey

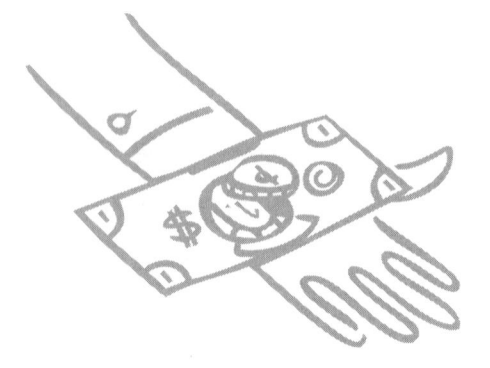

$1.50 for each book. Even that is a lot for some kids, so there's a layaway plan that allows kids to pay a little each week until a book is paid off.

Every fourth- and fifth-grade student at P.S. 121 is eligible to work at the bookstore, but first they have to apply and be hired by Mrs. Cohen.

Every Tuesday and Thursday morning, before school, the stock clerks busily put out all the books and displays. When the store opens, the security guards place themselves at the doors to control the large number of students and their parents who come to browse and buy. The cashiers use their math skills and calculators to add up purchases. And advertising execs paint colorful posters and banners to advertise the store. The staff are paid with certificates at the end of each month, if they came to work (on time!) and did their jobs. They use the certificates to buy their own books at the store.

"In third grade I visited the Children's Bookstore almost every Tuesday and Thursday," says Bharati Kemraj. "When I got to fourth grade, Mrs. Cohen gave out applications to the children who wanted to work in the bookstore. I applied for a job. I wanted to do a cashier job. After giving my application to Mrs. Cohen, I had to go for an interview. Then I received an acceptance letter.

Working Girl

"Working in the bookstore is a lot of fun. Sometimes it's hard because a lot of parents, children, and teachers come to buy books. The best part of working in the bookstore is getting paid with free books. The bookstore is the best place to buy books."

In 1997, nearly 8 million American women owned businesses, and the number is increasing.

HIGH PROFILE: JANET BROWN

The U.S. Department of Labor estimates that only 4,900 out of 819,000 automobile mechanics in the United States are women. One female mechanic is Janet Brown, the owner of the Women's Auto Clinic in Newport News, Virginia.

New Moon: When did you first get interested in a career as an auto mechanic?

Janet Brown: It was about five years ago. I was looking for a position in something where women had not yet entered a man's field, and where I could give more jobs to women.

NM: What's it like to own your own business?

JB: It's very, very hard. It's very difficult because you are in an all-male field. You have to be very strong, and it's very expensive. But I'm proud of it.

NM: Is it hard to be a woman pursuing a career that is thought of as a "man's job"?

JB: Most definitely. You have to have experience. I've been an entrepreneur for thirty-seven years. I've owned many businesses. Experience is the thing that you have to have in owning a business like this because challenging a man's field is very difficult. First, people think you're a joke. Second, people do not want to respect that you really do know what you are doing. You have to prove it each time, until they are your regular customers.

NM: What is your favorite part of your job?

JB: I like to talk with the customers about their cars. My knowledge of cars helps me talk to them. But I am a better businessperson than a mechanic, so I do what I do best — run the business.

Working Girl

NM: How many people work in your shop?

JB: We have five mechanics, and they all are women. I just hired an 18-year-old — she's the youngest one I've had here. She won't be finished with her mechanic's course until June, but she seems to be doing real good.

NM: Do female mechanics communicate better than males with their clients?

JB: Yes, definitely. It's often very hard for a woman to describe a problem with her car, except by describing a noise. Women can tell us if their cars are "clinging" or "clacking" or whatever the noise is, and we understand. We are tuned in to each other. A male may look at women like, "What do you mean — a noise?" Our customer numbers are growing by leaps and bounds because we have that communication.

NM: Are most of your clients men or women?

JB: When we first started, about three and a half years ago, it was about ninety percent male and ten percent female. But now it's pretty equal. I'm real proud that women come in here and that men are very happy with us, too. Men say that they feel like I could treat their car the same way they do — with a little bit of kindness.

—Rachel, age 11, Minnesota

Working Girl

Baby-sitting

Baby-sitting is a great way to make money if you love kids. (You can tell all your mom and dad's friends with babies about your baby-sitting service for their future needs.) You can do fun art projects and play sports and games with the children. Lauren says, "Something I like doing on rainy days or nights is making cookies with the kids I baby-sit. You can learn a lot about yourself and your patience, and about kids."

The amount of money you may receive for baby-sitting varies from area to area and from family to family. Some sitters charge an additional sum — say, 50 cents an hour — for more than two children. Some charge $1 more per hour after 11 o'clock. It really depends on you and the family. Flynn, for example, baby-sits every Thursday for the parents of two young kids and is paid about $13 for watching the children from 6 to 8:30 P.M. She adds, "It's important not to just lounge in front of MTV all night with the kids. Play games or read books with them."

Before you get started, check around your community to find baby-sitting and first aid classes — it's important to know the basics!

Working Girl

Ask a Girl

"There are two families who keep asking me to baby-sit. One of them pays me twice as much as the other one. The problem is that I like the kids in the lower-paying family better. In fact, the other kids give me a headache!"

This is not something that I can decide for you. Do you need the money badly? How often would you be baby-sitting the annoying children? Benjamin Franklin once said, "Time is money." How much is your time worth?

Pet-sitting

I am a regular pet-sitter for two families in our town. Whenever either of them goes away, they rely on me to care for their cats. I also walk a wonderful dog every day after school and get paid $10 a week. Because most people adore and love their pets, they normally don't trust a stranger with their "babies." Therefore, it's hard to get a job caring for animals merely by advertising your services. All of the jobs I've gotten have been through word of mouth.

Working Girl

This situation is ideal for me, because I get a chance to interact with animals whom I love, and I get money desperately needed for all that junk I can't live without.

—Flynn, age 11, New York

Cleaning House

I sometimes make extra money by cleaning our basement and our porch. How much I get depends on how messy the place is. If I cleaned it every week, I would get about $1. The good things about doing the job are that I have money to get presents for other people, and once in a while, I get something for myself. The bad thing is sometimes I get hurt—I got splinters once. Also, you can't play while you are doing the job. If I needed to earn even more money, I could ask my grandma or my aunt if I could clean for her.

Of course, sometimes it is nice to clean for free. Once I cleaned the whole upstairs of our house, and I made cookies. The house was messy—really messy. I did that for free. My mom never even knew I was doing it until it was all done, though she was kind of suspicious because it took over four hours (that tells you how messy it was!). When

Working Girl

she saw, she said, "Ahhhhhh." Sometimes the best pay is making someone happy.

—Ashley, age 10, Minnesota

More Ways to Make Money

Well, we hope you've gotten some good ideas already. Here's a list of even more to think about or try—be creative and personalize each job to fit you.

- Home-office help
- Catering
- Computer-game tester
- Camp counselor
- Web site design
- Oil changing
- Window washing
- Floor cleaning
- Rug shampoo service
- Paper route
- Housecleaning
- Gift-wrapping service
- Wake-up and reminder calls
- Selling handmade mailboxes
- Ironing
- Recovering lost golf balls
- Pet washing
- Selling handmade cards
- Fence painting
- Making and selling buttons
- Candy making
- Tutoring
- Selling flowers or plants
- Pet portraits
- Giving music lessons
- Running children's parties

Made your first million yet? (We mean pennies, of course. Let's see, how many dollars would a million pennies make anyway?)

Volunteering

Working for money is great if you need some funds, but volunteering is a blast, too. You can help a cause that you believe in by donating time instead of (or in addition to) money. And there are hundreds of different volunteer opportunities — you don't have to be cooped up addressing letters all day. If you like little kids, you could do story hours at your local library; if you love animals, you could help a vet or work at an animal shelter; and if you really get into volunteering, you could skip summer camp and go be an assistant to biologists studying coral reefs in the South Pacific.

Not only does volunteer work make you feel good and look great on college applications, it can get you a job in the future. You get valuable experience and personal connections if you volunteer in the field that you plan to make your career.

Volunteering in your community is one of the best things you can do for yourself and others. "When I help my community," Lauren says, "I'm happy knowing that I helped something or someone in need."

There are many ways and opportunities to help your community. You can volunteer at a community organization, or you can even start your own club. Lauren started a

Working Girl

club on Kauai called the Kids Helping Kids Club. They've worked a lot with the Salvation Army and even have undertaken their own ventures to help the community. Lauren also works with the children at the YWCA women's shelter.

You can call up any nonprofit organization in the community and ask the staff if they need volunteers for an upcoming event. They'd probably love your help and could use it. You should try giving some of your time to your community. Lauren says, "You'll be surprised how much happiness you'll get out of it, how much people will appreciate your help, and how much it will help them."

Twelve-year-old Cynthia Landon and her friend Kymberleigh Bell agree with Lauren. They created Kids for Habitat in their hometown, Hammond, Louisiana. Kids for Habitat helps raise money for Habitat for Humanity, an international organization that builds homes for — and with — poor people.

HIGH PROFILE: CYNTHIA LANDON

New Moon: Tell us about Kids for Habitat.

Cynthia Landon: One day, my friend Kym was over at

my house, and she said that we should do something to earn money for Habitat for Humanity. There are laws that say kids can't help build houses, so we raise money instead. We got some seashells and painted them with fingernail polish. We sold them for 25 cents each at church. We did other little things like that, and then I called some friends to start a group: Kids for Habitat. At our meetings, we think of fund-raisers and we work out how to make them happen.

NM: How many people are in your group?

CL: Right now, there are 14 kids in Kids for Habitat. We are between the ages of 8 and 15.

NM: Tell us about the different fund-raisers and projects you've had.

CL: First we sold seashells. We've also had a bake sale, a garage sale, and a car wash. We pick projects from a list of needs that the local Habitat for Humanity has. They also gave us a list of houses that need to be built around the world. We're paying for a house to be built in Honduras. It costs about $500 to build a house there.

NM: How long did it take Kids for Habitat to raise the money to build one house?

CL: We had a bake sale in April, and we had a garage sale in May. With those two events, we raised more than $1,000. Many families donated stuff to our garage sale. Some people brought over truckloads of stuff for us to sell.

NM: What is your favorite part of raising money to build homes?

CL: I know that for each house built, it is one less family who is living on the street. That makes me feel good. My dad told me once that there are people who live in boxes instead of homes. I have a lot compared to those people, and I want to give some of what I have back.

—Nina, age 11, and Kerri, age 14, Minnesota

Working Girl

Ask a Girl

"I want to volunteer for an animal shelter, but I also need to make money and keep up with my schoolwork, soccer team, and social life! What can I do?"

That sounds like an annoying situation! It can be awful trying to juggle so many aspects of your life. But it is something that you're always going to need to know how to do for the rest of your life. Why don't you get a job? There are tons of ideas in this book, so find something you like and get working! You could do homework at a set time, say, starting right after dinner. You could volunteer once a week (if you have time, otherwise once every two weeks or once a month). And you can even try coordinating your volunteer time with friends.

Ask yourself whether you really need to take on a job at this point, or if you would prefer to spend more of your time with your friends performing volunteer work.

Working Girl

Yaquana Madyun is another dedicated girl, who gets together with other kids and adults in her neighborhood in Boston, Massachusetts, to clean up vacant lots and parks. She also spends part of her summers raising food on a farm outside the city.

HIGH PROFILE: YAQUANA MADYUN

New Moon: What do you get out of working on cleanup projects?

Yaquana Madyun: You feel good when you see how your community has changed and you know that you helped it. I like to help clean my own community to make it look better so that I can enjoy it and my younger brother can enjoy it and all the little kids who are still growing up can enjoy it.

NM: How much time do you spend working on this?

YM: In the summer, I work on a farm in Lincoln, outside Boston, and we do a lot of community service here in Boston. We plant vegetables and pick them, and we bring them to homeless shelters. There are also city people who buy shares of the crop, and we sell the food we grow to them. I've met a lot of different people there, and it is nice to communicate with them. On weekends, we have different neighborhood cleanups. We get together and decide different things that we can do.

NM: What are the cleanups like? Who comes to them, and what do you do?

YM: Anyone who wants to can come — adults, kids, and people just bring their friends. We pick out certain vacant lots that have a lot of trash in them, and a group of people goes to each one of them and cleans up the trash and weeds and makes it look nicer. Basically all of my friends and my whole family are involved in it, so we do it together.

NM: So you have fun cleaning up?

YM: Yes. We even have cookouts afterward, and games and prizes.

NM: What do your classmates think about this?

YM: A lot of people who aren't used to this say, "Wow. It's a lot of work. How can you go out and do this all the time, cleaning up and everything?" But they actually think it is pretty cool that I do go out.

NM: Do you like living in your neighborhood now? Is it a better place to live than when you were younger?

YM: Yes, definitely. I've lived here all my life, but I've moved into a better house. They filled up a lot of the vacant lots with houses. It looks much better now.

NM: How does it make you feel to see that change?

YM: I can't explain the feeling; it's great. I've grown up seeing all these people work so hard for it, and when it finally happens, it's just the greatest feeling.

NM: Does your group make any efforts to spread the idea of what you do to other communities?

YM: Yes. It's word of mouth. Your friends tell other people, and they form different youth groups in other places.

How to Manage Your Money

CHAPTER THREE

Okay, now that you've figured out how and why to get money, it's time to put your cash to work! In this chapter, we look at budgets and banks, spending and saving, and even the stock market!

Your Secret Weapon: A Budget

Money is a trading tool — you give money, and you receive a service or an object. Money isn't much help just sitting around. Now, you could go and blow all of your money on those trendy new shoes. But that means you'd have to go out and earn more right away. You can spend your money more carefully, but that requires some planning. This is called budgeting.

There are many ways to budget. When you save at least $1 a week, that's budgeting. It's also budgeting to put half of your income aside until you save enough for your new shoes. (Income is how much cash you get over a certain period of time — daily, weekly, or annually.)

Making a system for what to do with your money means taking a simple first step: Look at your *needs* versus your *wants*. Most of us don't yet support ourselves, so we don't have to pay for most of our basic necessities, like rent or groceries, insurance or taxes. Even if you do have to help out with those expenses, write down all the stuff you spend money on: books, gifts, candy, jewelry, amusement, clothes, movies, music, pets, food, skin care. From the big list, pick the things you absolutely have to buy, such as lunch at school or underwear. This is your "needs" list. Everything else is a "want." Adults and businesses often divide expenses the same way; they call their needs "fixed expenses" and their wants "nonfixed expenses," which they pay for with "disposable income."

Now, to get an idea of what you spend, keep a "spending diary" for a week. Have a notebook and a pen or a pencil in your purse, your backpack, or whatever you carry around. Every time you buy something, write the item down in the notebook, along with the date, its price, and where you bought it. Write down everything you spend, no matter how small or unimportant it seems (that $1 pen and 75-cent can of soda add up). At the end of the week, look at your record of everything you bought. You may be surprised at how much all those small purchases end up costing you. If you're surprised, you may want to repeat the diary for another week. If you think you did a good job with your spending, celebrate, or at least congratulate yourself. It's not easy resisting your temptations to buy things.

How to Manage Your Money

If, on the other hand, you're not happy when you find out where your money went, then you might want to fill out an actual budget. Here's one type of budget form you can try for yourself:

Weekly Income

Allowance _____

Pay from any jobs _____

Other income (might include
savings account interest or cash gifts) _____

Total income per week _____

Weekly Expenses

Needs (expenses that stay about the same)

Transportation _____

Lunch _____

Savings and investments _____

Dues

    Girl Scouts _____

    Youth group _____

    Organizations you support _____

How to Manage Your Money

Wants (expenses that vary)

Food (snacks) _____
Clothing _____
Entertainment
    Movies _____
    Concerts _____
    CDs _____
    Video rentals _____
    Sports events _____
Magazines, books, etc. _____
Gifts for family and friends _____
Donations/charities _____

Total expenses per week _____

The goal of any budget is to get the amount of your total expenses to stay less than or at least the same as the amount of your income.

POINT OF VIEW: *Foreign Affairs*

When I was in Europe, I had to budget myself since I had $350 for the whole month and a lot of souvenirs and gifts to buy. To make matters worse, there was the difference in currency. In France the rate of exchange was 6 francs to a dollar. So it wasn't that hard to do the math. But in Spain, it was 160 pesetas to a dollar. Now, 100 is a pretty large number in American money, but in pesetas that's not even a dollar. So when I went shopping and saw prices like 640 pesetas, that was 4 dollars. But forgetting the difference in currency, I was thinking, "Whoa, this stuff is high-priced." So I ended up missing out on a lot of nice things because of my mistake.

—Morgan, age 12, Washington, D.C.

Savings

A smart budget has one more category: savings. Think about it: Do you have to pay, or help pay, for a car or college in the relatively near future? Do you want to go to a summer camp or help pay for music lessons? The only way to save is to figure out *ahead* of time — that is, before you spend all your money — what portion of your money to put away toward whatever you're saving up for. (We've been looking for a way that lets us save all our money and spend it all at the same time. Sorry to say, no luck yet!)

One way to save money is to put the amount you don't need or want to spend in the bank and keep the rest of your cash at home. Flynn knows a girl who has a box each for Outings, Music, Charity, Clothes, and Car. Whenever she gets any money, she puts it in one of these boxes. Then when she, say, wants a CD, all she has to do is see if there's enough money in the Music box. Instant budget!

But what about the money you don't want to keep around? Here's where those banks come in. They make it simple to stash away money in a savings account. First, your money is safe because it's really hard to steal money from a bank (and if someone does, the bank's insurance pays you back). Plus, keeping your money in a bank can earn you *interest*. Interest is the money a bank pays you for keeping your money with it—you don't have to do anything else but make deposits. Banks usually pay anywhere from 3 to 5 percent, which may seem like a little, but once your savings are larger—say, $3,000—you'll make a lot. If your bank pays 5 percent interest and you have $1,000 in your account, you'll earn $50 in interest annually.

Basically, interest is the payment on money that has been borrowed. When you put money into a savings account, the bank is "borrowing" it, so the bank pays you interest. If you borrow money as a loan (for a car, college, a small business, or a house), then the amount you borrow includes the interest that you have to pay back. So if you borrow $10,000 at 5 percent, you have to pay back $10,000, plus $500 per year.

How do you know what kind of account is best for you? Most people keep their money in a combination of a checking account and some form of savings account. A checking account is a bank account that allows you to write out an order—a check—to pay for something. Checking accounts are used to cover basic expenses, like rent or mortgage payments, telephone and electricity/heating bills, transportation, clothing, and food, as well as small entertainment items.

How to Manage Your Money

Most banks will link your checking and savings accounts. Often this means that you will earn interest on the total amount of money you have combined in both accounts.

To open an account, you'll need to have your Social Security number and usually a parent's signature on file. Some states require an adult to be on any account for someone under the age of 18.

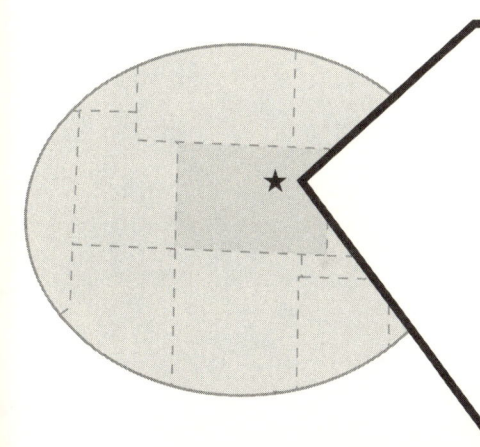

> The Young Americans Bank in Denver offers savings and checking accounts for anyone up to age 22. Its address is 250 Steele Street, Denver, Colorado 80206. Telephone: (303) 321-2265. www.theyoungamericans.org

To write a check to someone, you fill in the name of the person or the company on the line that says "Pay to the order of..." In a box next to that line, you write a dollar amount in numbers — say, $25.50 — and on the line below, you spell out the amount, such as "Twenty-five and $^{50}/_{100}$." In the upper right corner, you put in the date, and in the lower right corner, you sign your name. What if you've sent out a check and the company never receives it or you have a problem? For a fee, you can tell the bank to stop payment on that particular check so it can never be cashed.

To make a deposit, you can use a special preprinted slip that the bank supplies when you open a checking account, or you can use a blank bank deposit slip and fill in that information. If a check from someone else is made out to you, be sure to sign your name on the back and write "for deposit only" and your bank account number. That way, if you lose the check, no one else will be able to cash it.

Whenever you write out a check or make a deposit, fill in the amount in your checkbook and subtract it from or add it to your balance so you know exactly how much money is left in your account. Once a month, compare the balance in your checkbook with the balance on the account statement that the bank sends you. The two balances should match, but they might not because you may have written checks after the statement's end date. If that's the case, you'll need to figure out which checks haven't been included on your statement and then subtract their amounts from the bank's balance. You might have to add interest, if you've earned any, and subtract any bank fees. And if you find a mistake in the bank's calculations, contact them to get it corrected.

How to Manage Your Money

Ask a Girl

"What is an ATM? Can I use one myself?"

"ATM" stands for "automatic teller machine," and there are ATMs worldwide now. If you can get an ATM card for your bank account, you can withdraw money even when the bank is closed or far away. You go to a machine and insert your card. Then you enter your PIN (personal identification number). You key in how much money you want, and it comes directly out of your bank account. The money is usually in multiples of $20. Finally you receive your money, and your card is returned. Some ATMs can take deposits also.

> More and more I am certain that the only difference between man and animals is that men can count and animals cannot and if they count they mostly do count money.
>
> —Gertrude Stein

POINT OF VIEW: *Bank on It*

To open a bank account by yourself, you must be 18. Before you're that age, you can open one with your parents as "custodians." I have an account at our town's bank. I put in $5 after I get my allowance. I put money in the first week of every month. I think it's good to have a schedule of when to put in money and not to do it miscellaneously. Every time I put money in, I get a receipt. Every once in a while, I get a statement (like a letter) in the mail that tells me how much interest I got, how much money I put in since the last statement, and the grand total.

—Katie, age 11, Minnesota

From Main Street to Wall Street

How can you make your money grow? One way is to invest it by buying stocks. A stock consists of one or more shares of a company, so when you buy it, you own part of the company. A company sells stock to people and uses the money to help the company grow. The value of the stock goes up and down depending on how much people are willing to pay for it, how well the company is doing, or how well the world's economy is doing.

A fun way to jump into the stock market is by starting an investment club with your friends. Shopping for stocks is like shopping for anything else. Make a list of all the products you like and use — jeans, shoes, shampoo, candy, etc. Then, with your friends, study the companies that make these products to see which ones are doing well and coming out with great new products and which ones are not doing well. You also might want to research which companies are polluters, which have women in important jobs, and which pay their workers decent wages. When you've found a company that you like, and your research shows that it seems to be getting better every year, then you and your friends can buy some of its stock as a group.

How to Manage Your Money

You can start investing with as little as $10, but most stocks cost more. A share in GirlCo, Inc., might sell for $22 one week and $28 the next week. If you bought one share for $22 and sold it when the price rose to $28, you would make $6. However, if you bought the share for $28 and the price dropped to $22, you would lose $6 if you sold the stock. Over time, the value of most stocks goes up. But don't forget: if you use a broker, she'll charge you a commission.

The way stocks grow is calculated in percentages. If the GirlCo, Inc., stock grew by 10% in a year, a $22 share would become worth $24.20. $22 x 10% = $22 x .10 = $2.20 — which is added to the original price of $22 to get $24.20!

The cool thing about investing when you are young is that there is more time for your money to make money. Over time, invested money compounds. Compounding is when the money you first invested earns money, and then you earn money on that new total. Remember the $2.20 that the GirlCo, Inc., stock earned? The next time the stock grows by 10%, you earn $2.42, because that's 10% of $24.20 (your new total). $24.20 x 10% = $24.20 x .10 = $2.42 — add that to $24.20 and you get $26.62. Compounding makes the amount you originally invested grow fast, so the sooner you start, the more you can earn!

How to Manage Your Money

Ask a Girl

> "I get a decent allowance from my parents, but I never seem to have enough money when I want to buy something or go out with my friends. Help!"

Allowances are wonderful. However, when they fall short, you may want to get a job. See Chapter Two for lots of ideas. If you don't have time for a job, brainstorm ideas for fun things you can do with friends for little or no money. Perhaps you could take the train or bus somewhere and explore (for a few dollars or less). Or you and a friend could volunteer at the local preschool or soup kitchen.

Allowance

What do you think is a fair amount to get for an allowance? The average weekly amount for kids ages 9 to 12 is $5, according to a survey in *Zillions* magazine. Thirteen- and fourteen-year-olds get slightly more, about $6 a week. How much you get is probably your main concern, but here are other allowance issues that you might want to discuss with your parents:

- *When will I be paid?* If you get paid on Friday night, will you spend your whole allowance by Monday and not have money for lunch? If payday is Sunday night, you can't go right to a store and blow it.
- *How will I be paid?* Decide whether you'd like your money in cash and, if so, in what denominations. You have a few choices: one big five-dollar bill, or five singles, or four singles and four quarters. Would you be less likely to break a large bill or more likely to save four singles and spend only one?
- *How often will I be paid?* Once a week is the most common schedule, but it's not the only one. Some kids really like being paid monthly or even quarterly (four times a year). That way they have to budget and plan more, and they learn faster how to manage money. Also, they don't have to bug their parents as often. Of course, whatever schedule you use, you have to know yourself and how well your schedule will fit your money-management strengths and weaknesses.
- *What will I be paid for?* Families seem pretty split on what allowances are for and why kids should get them. Some believe allowances are paid in exchange

for kids performing regular chores, so the kids learn about earning their pay. But other families think this method teaches kids to expect to be paid for any help they offer. Those families pay allowances without tying work directly to the money. They expect their kids to pitch in because they're part of the family, not because they're going to be paid. The bottom line: Make sure you and the person paying your allowance agree about what your allowance and any household duties mean.

◆ *What will happen if I don't fulfill my end of the bargain?* Ask your parents ahead of time what they expect of you and exactly what will happen to your allowance if you don't do it. You can avoid arguments this way; plus, you'll be less likely to forget what you are supposed to do.

How to Manage Your Money

Ask a Girl

> *"My parents are divorced, and my mom and I depend on my dad for money. I have two problems. First, I don't want to wind up like my mom and not be able to earn a living. And second, right now she doesn't have enough money to spare any for an allowance for me, so I never have enough to do fun stuff with my friends."*

Women in past generations usually did not have much (or any) control over money. But girls like us want to be in charge. If you want to be financially responsible, practice. Get a job and budget your money. Learn how to pay for some of the stuff you want. Open a bank account. It is not only adults who can use real-life things like banks and ATMs. Start now, and when you are grown up, you will be financially responsible. Also, if you earn your own money now, you won't need an allowance. ◇

POINT OF VIEW: *Tips on Allowances*

An allowance is important for growing up. It helps you learn to handle money responsibly and gives you money for the things that you need when you can't get a real job.

There are two ways to get an allowance from your parents. One way is that your parents make up the weekly, monthly, or even yearly rate of your allowance and they are the decision makers, period. The other way is for you to negotiate with your parents and be part of setting the amount. I would have to go with the second way because it is better for your own good. Remember, when negotiating with your parents, don't raise your voice, don't be disrespectful, and don't forget to listen with an open mind. Do talk rationally; be respectful of your parents' side, too; and don't complain if the outcome isn't what you wanted.

A lot of parents have their kids do chores (such as cleaning their room, vacuuming once every two weeks, feeding and taking care of the pets, etc.) in return for their allowances. If you don't do your chores or the things that you need to do to get your allowance, then your parents might skip your allowance for that time. That is your consequence to face and the outcome of your very own decisions.

Some parents just give their kids allowances and they don't require chores, but they wouldn't mind if the kids helped out once in a while. Right now I get $5 every Sunday, and I'm not required to do any chores, so that is good for me. I have raised my allowance by negotiating with my parents and telling them how I feel. I am going to get a raise again pretty soon because I just had a meeting/negotiating time with my parents about my allowance.

—Julia, age 14, Minnesota

Fun with Money

CHAPTER FOUR

Fun with Money

Spending money is almost always fun. But there are scads of other ways to enjoy the green stuff — not to mention the silver, gold, nickel, and even copper stuff!

Money Club

Try forming a money club with some of your friends. Once a week, everyone in the club brings a set amount of money — say, two to five dollars — to a meeting. Put everyone's money together and give it to one person to spend. If you were doing this with three friends, then each of you would get a turn once a month.

You could have a rule that the money has to be spent on something important, something you've wanted for a long time. For example, you wouldn't just go out and buy a ton of candy, but you could get a book you love or a pair of pants that you think are really cool. You could use the money to go to a live concert by your favorite rock group, or to order their CD instead. Be creative.

Your club can also try variations like spending your pooled money on something you then share. Wouldn't it be fun to buy a new video game, or maybe hire a guitar

Fun with Money

teacher for a group lesson? Or you could start investing your money in the stock market together. Students around the country have been forming investment clubs and have learned a lot while earning good returns on their investments.

Dollars and Sense Quiz

How many of these terms can you define? You're a money whiz if you know ten or more! If you get stuck, check the glossary (pp. 84–86) in the resource section.

balance	401(k)	return
bankruptcy	gross income	risk
bond	inflation	salary
budget	interest	savings
capital	investment	statement
checking	loan	stock
collateral	mutual fund	wages
credit	net income	withdrawal
deposit	premium	
expenses	profit	

Fun with Money

The Rich Grandmother Game

If you want to learn about the stock market, get into it!

In the Rich Grandmother Game, you pretend that you had a grandmother who died and left you $10,000. You must "invest" the money in stocks of real companies. To choose stocks, think of products and businesses that you and your friends like. Follow your stocks in your daily newspaper. Use a notebook to record how much each of your stocks gains or loses every day. Then, after a week or a month, see how much money you have "made." It is very interesting to find out how the stock market works. Since it's only pretending, you won't lose any real money or, even worse, lose your grandmother!

Try the online version at library.advanced.org/3096.

Concrete Currency

Money, when we use it to buy stuff, is technically known as "currency." About nine thousand years ago, people used cattle for currency. Money made of metal didn't appear until much later, about 2000 B.C., in the form of bronze ingots. By about 1000 B.C., bronze gave way to silver and gold cat heads, statuettes of rulers or deities, or simply medallions.

The first uniform currency to be made in large amounts was produced in Anatolia (the part of Turkey now known as Asia Minor), in about 800 B.C. The currency was crude, bean-shaped pieces of electrum, a natural alloy of gold and silver.

In 640 B.C., the Lydians (who lived in part of Asia Minor) made the first true coins. Also made of electrum, they had animals or faces of men imprinted on them.

The Chinese experimented with paper currency around 1 B.C. However, paper money did not come to the Western world until the early eighteenth century, in France.

In the highlands of Irian Jaya, the Indonesian half of New Guinea, cowrie shells are used as money. They're very valuable because the natives live so far from the ocean.

Decoding American Currency

American money holds many secrets. The pyramid on the back of the one-dollar bill is no exception. Francis Hopkinson, who signed the Declaration of Independence and designed the U.S. flag, decided on the pyramid as a fitting symbol to appear on U.S. currency.

The top of the pyramid is unfinished, which symbolizes that the U.S. is never finished, that we are still perfecting our country. The Roman numerals MDCCLXXVI on the pyramid's base are 1776, the year we declared independence. The caption below the pyramid, *Novus Ordo Seclorum,* is Latin for "a new order of the ages." The eye hovering above the pyramid also has a caption, *Annuit Coeptis,* Latin for "He favors our undertakings."

The first portrait to appear on an American bill was that of Secretary of the Treasury Salmon P. Chase. Later, in 1886, Martha Washington became the first and only woman whose portrait has adorned paper currency. The United States didn't use faces and portraits on coins until 1909, the centennial of Lincoln's birth, when his portrait was put on the penny. In 1932, two hundred years after George Washington's birth, our first president was honored on the quarter.

Fun with Money

Monopoly

Make your own board game involving "play" money and tough decisions. You can base your game on one such as Monopoly™, Pay Day™, or Hot Company, a board game from Independent Means. Or you can create one from scratch. Include scenarios that will bring out the best in an aspiring female entrepreneur. Use bright colors and get creative!

Barter Buddies

Bartering, or trading stuff without cash involved, can be a blast *and* a huge help for your budget. How does it work? Any way you want it to, really. You find a friend or a group of friends who agree to exchange "goods and services" with each other. For example, you need someone to walk your dog while you're away for the weekend. You ask your barter buddy if she will do it in exchange for your giving her extra help with her math homework for a week. Or you trade material possessions, like: I'll trade you my earrings for your book, or blouse, or video, or... You get the idea. It helps to get together once in a while and make a list of all the kinds of things you could barter with each other.

If you're really ambitious, you can start bartering with

Fun with Money

your parents and even with people in your community. Think about it: Wouldn't it be cool to trade raking the neighbor's lawn for a piano lesson, or washing the car for a ride to the mall?

You can also hold a barter party. Invite your friends to bring anything they'd like to trade or give away, pile it all in the middle of the living room, and dig in! You know what they say: One girl's discards are another girl's treasures! A variation on this theme is to have each girl write a service she is willing to offer on a slip of paper and then trade with another girl. Examples: returning library books, baking cookies, cleaning her room, sewing on a button, decorating a pair of jeans, French-braiding her hair.

> For a dollar bill to be usable, it must be at least three-quarters complete or have the entire serial number intact.

Fun with Money

Currency Quiz

Can you match the kind of currency used in each country?
(See page 86 for answers!)

Country

Australia
Brazil
China
Czech Republic
Denmark
Ethiopia
France
Germany
Ghana
Great Britain
Greece
Haiti
India
Israel
Italy
Japan
Jordan
Laos
Malaysia
Mexico
Mongolia
Morocco
The Netherlands
Peru
Poland
Portugal
Russia
Saudi Arabia
South Africa
South Korea
Spain
Sweden
Thailand
United States
Venezuela
Zambia

Currency

tugrik
drachma
dollar
zloty
koruna
cedi
birr
rupee
franc
gourde
cruzeiro
bolivar
deutsche mark
guilder
ruble
yen
baht
kip
ringgit
peseta
yuan
dirham
shekel
inti
krone
lira
escudo
dollar
rand
kwacha
peso
krona
dinar
riyal
pound
won

Finding Out More About Money

CHAPTER FIVE

Finding Out More About Money

A comprehensive list of resources for New Moon girls to keep exploring and having fun with money and work:

Books (Fiction)

Ballet Shoes by Noel Streatfeild (Random House, 1995)

Charlie Pippin by C. D. Boyd (Viking Press, 1988)

A Dragon in the Cliff by Sheila Cole (Lothrop, Lee & Shepard, 1991)

A Girl of the Limberlost by Gene Stratton Porter (Indiana University Press, 1987)

Henry and the Paper Route by Beverly Cleary (William Morrow & Co. Library, 1987)

His Majesty, Queen Hatshepsut by Dorothy Carter (Lippincott-Raven, 1987)

Lyddie by Katherine Paterson (Puffin, 1994)

The Midwife's Apprentice by Karen Cushman (HarperTrophy, 1996)

Not for a Billion Gazillion Dollars by Paula Danziger (Paper Star, 1998)

Oh, Those Harper Girls! by Kathleen Karr (Sunburst, 1995)

Books (Nonfiction)

Dr. Tightwad's Money-Smart Kids by Janet Bodnar (Kiplinger, 1997)

Fast Cash for Kids by Bonnie and Noel Drew (Career Press, Inc., 1995)

50 Money Making Ideas for Kids by Larry Burkett (Thomas Wilson, 1997)

Girls and Young Women Inventing by Frances A. Karnes, Ph.D., and Suzanne M. Bean, Ph.D. (Free Spirit Press, 1995)

Finding Out More About Money

Investing for Life: A Simple Guide to Investments and Personal Finance for Teenagers by the National Association of Investors Corporation (NAIC, 1997)

Jobs for Kids: The Guide to Having Fun and Making Money by Carol Barkin (Lothrop, Lee & Shepard, 1990)

Kid Cash: Creative Money-Making Ideas (For Kids by Kids) by Joe Lamancusa (Tab Books, 1993)

The Kids' Allowance Book by Amy Nathan (Walker and Co., 1998)

The Kids' Business Book by Arlene Erlbach (Walker and Co., 1998)

No More Frogs to Kiss: 99 Ways to Give Economic Power to Girls by Joline Godfrey (Harperbusiness, 1995)

101 Marvelous Money-Making Ideas for Kids by Heather Wood (Tor Books, 1995)

Our Wildest Dreams: Women Entrepreneurs Making Money, Having Fun, Doing Good by Joline Godfrey (Harperbusiness, 1993)

Show Me the Money! 101 Money Making Projects for Kids by Bonnie Drew (Summit Financial Products, 1998)

Students Shopping for a Better World by the Council on Economic Priorities (Ballantine, 1993)

Teenage Money Making Guide by Allan Smith (Success Advertising and Publishing, 1984)

The Totally Awesome Business Book for Kids: With Twenty Super Businesses You Can Start Right Now! by Adriane G. Berg and Arthur Berg Bochner (Newmarket Press, 1993)

The Ultimate Kids' Club Book: How to Organize, Find Members, Run Meetings, Raise Money, Handle Problems, and Much More! by Melissa Maupin and Rosemary Wallner (Free Spirit, 1996)

Finding Out More About Money

Magazines

NEW MOON
P.O. Box 3587
Duluth, MN 55803-3587
(800) 381-4743

KIDS' WALL STREET NEWS
P.O. Box 1207
Rancho Santa Fe, CA 92067
(619) 633-1182

MONEY
P.O. Box 60001
Tampa, FL 33660
(800) 633-9970

THE WALL STREET JOURNAL CLASSROOM EDITION
Dept. 6AAT
P.O. Box 7019
Chicopee, MA 01021-7019
(800) 544-0522, ext. 6AAT

YOUNG MONEY MATTERS MAGAZINE
711 W. Thirteen Mile Rd.
Madison Heights, MI 48071
(248) 583-6242

ZILLIONS
P.O. Box 54861
Boulder, CO 80322
(800) 388-5626

Internet

www.newmoon.org
The inside scoop on New Moon, with stories from the magazine, contests, and other fun interactive features.

www.better-investing.org/youth/youth.html
Sponsored by the National Association of Investors Corporation, the site has lots of interesting articles on the stock market and investment clubs for young people.

www.girlsinc.org/money
This cool site has interactive games, a time line on women and money, and good definitions of financial terms.

www.independentmeans.com
The great Web site of the national organization An Income of Her Own, devoted to educating girls about business. Tons of useful stuff.

library.advanced.org/3096
This Web site is designed by kids for kids. It examines stocks, bonds, and mutual funds and has a stock market game.

www.ustreas.gov/kids
This is the U.S. Department of Treasury's page designed specifically for kids. You can get a virtual tour of where your money is actually *made,* and learn about who controls it and how the U.S. Treasury system works.

Finding Out More About Money

Glossary

annual report: a yearly financial report that a company's management sends to its shareholders.

balance: your earnings minus your expenses.

bankruptcy: the inability to meet your financial obligations, like paying your bills, rent, or mortgage.

blue chip stock: shares in any major company that pays its dividends reliably from year to year.

bond: an investment that provides a regular payment to its owner at a fixed rate of interest.

budget: a plan to save and spend your money, based on income and expenses.

capital: your financial assets — how much everything that you have is worth.

checking: a bank account from which you can draw funds easily — to pay bills, for example.

collateral: what a borrower has to pledge to get a loan; if the borrower can't repay the loan, her collateral will be taken in exchange.

credit: the power you have to borrow money, based on your financial history; the actual amount of money you borrow.

deposit: the money that you put into a checking or savings account.

dividend: a payment to a shareholder for his or her share of a company's profits.

expenses: the things you spend money on.

401(k): a type of pension plan that allows you to save money for retirement through your employer.

gross income: all the money you receive in earnings, interest,

Finding Out More About Money

and dividends before you subtract the money you have to pay for taxes and expenses.

gross profit: the amount of money, or income, made before any expenses (such as the cost of materials or taxes) are subtracted.

inflation: the rate at which the cost of goods and services in the economy increases from year to year.

interest: payment for money borrowed.

investment: a form of property (like a house or a stock) that you buy because you think it will become more valuable.

loan: money you borrow or lend.

money market fund: a mutual fund that invests in very secure money-earning properties, such as U.S. Treasury bills or bank certificates of deposit (CDs).

mutual fund: an investment that pools the financial resources of many investors to buy stocks, bonds, or money market funds.

net income: the money you have available after taxes and other expenses have been subtracted from gross income.

premium: payment for an insurance policy.

profit: earnings after the costs of making and selling a product or service are paid.

return: the amount of profit on an investment.

risk: the potential for loss of value on an investment (for example, something that's low-risk would protect your investment but might not give you a high rate of return, while something that is high-risk would offer a pretty high rate of return, but the potential to lose a large part of your investment also would be greater).

salary: the amount an employer pays you for your work.

savings: the amount of money you don't use on expenses.

Finding Out More About Money

statement: a description of income and expenses (for example, your bank statement would show you the deposits you put into an account and the checks you wrote in one month, while a company's statement would show its profits and losses).

stock: shares of ownership in a company.

stock exchange: a marketplace where people trade stocks and bonds. Two such marketplaces are the New York Stock Exchange and the American Stock Exchange.

taxes: money that the government collects on a portion of what people earn and spend.

wages: earnings from a job.

withdrawal: money you take out of a bank account.

Answers to quiz on page 79

Country	Currency	Country	Currency
Australia	dollar	Malaysia	ringgit
Brazil	cruzeiro	Mexico	peso
China	yuan	Mongolia	tugrik
Czech Republic	koruna	Morocco	dirham
Denmark	krone	The Netherlands	guilder
Ethiopia	birr	Peru	inti
France	franc	Poland	zloty
Germany	deutsche mark	Portugal	escudo
Ghana	cedi	Russia	ruble
Great Britain	pound	Saudi Arabia	riyal
Greece	drachma	South Africa	rand
Haiti	gourde	South Korea	won
India	rupee	Spain	peseta
Israel	shekel	Sweden	krona
Italy	lira	Thailand	baht
Japan	yen	United States	dollar
Jordan	dinar	Venezuela	bolivar
Laos	kip	Zambia	kwacha

🌸 New Moon Books Girls Editorial Board Biographies 🌸

Hi! My name is *Flynn Berry*. I'm 11 years old and live in a barely there, tiny teeny little speck-on-the-map suburb of New York City, New York. I love to write and create any form of art (collages, paintings, drawings, etc.). I am also interested in helping humans, including myself, stop hurting animals; playing soccer; karate; playing the flute; reading (particularly any Philip Pullman books, and anything by Madeleine L'Engle); exploring New York City; and spending time with my friends.

My name is *Lauren Noelani Calhoun,* and I am 13 years old. I live on the island of Kauai, Hawaii. I enjoy cooking, playing the oboe, hiking and camping, dancing, running, and spending time with friends. I have a service club called the Kids Helping Kids Club and volunteer at a women's shelter. I baby-sit whenever I get a chance, and I am learning to cook with a chef in a local restaurant. I hope to be a chef when I grow up, but we'll see!

My name is *Ashley Cofell*. I live in a small town in Minnesota. I'm 10 years old. I started writing books when I was seven or eight. I have written four books, which I have given to friends and family. I like to read short stories, especially scary ones. I also like to play soccer, swim, cook, ride my bike, go to the theater, and sing. I've been in two choirs. I want to be a writer and a doctor when I grow up.

My name is *Morgan Fykes*. I'm 12 years old, and I live in a large old house with a big porch and a room of my own in Washington, D.C. I'm in sixth grade at a private school for girls. I'm cheerful and I talk a lot, except when I'm meeting new people. My mom and I started a mother-daughter book club three years ago, and we wrote a book about the club. It was published last year, and I went on a book tour and did presentations on my own. I have an art section set up in one corner of my basement, and I also like dancing (tap, ballet, and jazz), sports, and camping.

My name is *Katie Hedberg*. I have a younger sister named Mollie and a younger brother named Sam. I also have an older half-brother named Daniel. I'm 11 years old and in sixth grade in Minnesota. I like to go shopping, hang with my friends, listen to CDs, read magazines, and do stuff that a normal 11-year-old would do. I play the piano and the trumpet and sing in choir. I had a chapter in the book *Girls Know Best*. I'm a Girl Scout and I help with my younger sister's troop.

My name is *Elizabeth Larsson* and I live near Philadelphia. Among many things, one of my passions is dancing. I love to dance, especially ballet. When I grow up, I probably want to go into the profession of sports medicine for dancers, or physical therapy. Other things I like to do are read, write, play on the computer, and anything that involves making something. I have my own business making silk eye pillows, filled with little seeds, to help you relax. My favorite foods are pizza, baked ziti, and chocolate. I go to an all-girls school, and I'm a Quaker. I'm in the seventh grade.

I'm *Priscilla Mendoza*. I like listening to music, being outdoors, traveling, and trying new things. Soccer, gymnastics, and basketball are some of my favorite sports. My favorite color is lavender. On rainy days I like to grab a couple of friends and veg out on the couch to a couple of comedy or horror flicks. I'm 11 and in the seventh grade. I live in a college town in northern California. Someday I hope to be a journalist, a lawyer, or the president of my very own company...who knows? (But for now I'll stick to baby-sitting.)

Julia Peters-Axtell is from a small city in Minnesota. I used to be on the *New Moon* magazine board but decided to try something new, like this! I'm in eighth grade at a public high school. I have a little sister—Emma—and my two parents, who I love to death. My favorite things are: my parents, guys, my sister, gum, my friends, my cats, music, cappuccino, and dances. I love all kinds of sports, but especially I enjoy soccer, track, and softball. I am on the JV soccer and track teams.

My name is *Caitlin Stern* and I live in a small town in Alaska. I unschool, which means that I choose what I learn and how I learn it. I've played the piano since I was five (I'm 13 now) and the recorder since I was eight. I'm also learning Japanese. I like jogging, biking, ice skating, and downhill skiing. I like to read books by Philip Pullman, Jules Verne, and Daniel Quinn. I listen to rock mostly, especially the Beatles and Sean Lennon. I'm a Libra. I love hanging out with my friends, but most of them don't live in Alaska. I have lived in a lot of different places, like New Zealand, Bali, Hawaii, and England.

THE NEW MOON BOOKS GIRLS EDITORIAL BOARD

BACK ROW, LEFT TO RIGHT: Julia Peters-Axtell, Katie Hedberg, Flynn Berry, Morgan Fykes, Lauren Calhoun, Caitlin Stern, Priscilla Mendoza

FRONT ROW: Elizabeth Larsson, Ashley Cofell

The first convening of the New Moon Books Girls Editorial Board
New York City
May 1998

Celebrate and empower girls and women with New Moon Publishing!

"New Moon Publishing has an agenda for girls and young women that's refreshingly different from mainstream corporate media. New Moon is building a community of girls and young women intent on saving their true selves. New Moon's magazines are a godsend for girls and young women, for their parents and the adults who care about them."

—**Mary Pipher, Ph.D.,** author of *Reviving Ophelia: Saving the Selves of Adolescent Girls*

New Moon: The Magazine for Girls and Their Dreams
Edited by girls ages 8–14, *New Moon* is an ad-free international bimonthly magazine that is a joy to read at any age!

New Moon Network: For Adults Who Care About Girls
Share the successes and strategies of a worldwide network of parents, teachers, and other adults committed to raising healthy, confident girls.

Between the Moon and You
A catalog of delightful gifts that celebrate and educate girls and women. Visit at www.newmooncatalog.com.

New Moon Education Division
A variety of interactive workshops and compelling speakers for conferences or conventions.

For information on any of these New Moon resources, contact:

New Moon Publishing
P.O. Box 3620
Duluth, MN 55803-3620
Toll-free: 800-381-4743 • Fax: 218-728-0314
E-mail: newmoon@newmoon.org
Web site: www.newmoon.org